Avocado Asks

For my mum,
who never asks what I am
—M.A.

All rights reserved. Published in the United States by Doubleday, an imprint of Random House Children's Books,
a division of Penguin Random House LLC, New York. Originally published in the United Kingdom by Orchard Books,
an imprint of Hachette Children's Group, part of The Watts Publishing Group Limited, London, in 2020.

Doubleday and the colophon are registered trademarks of Penguin Random House LLC.

Visit us on the Web! rhcbooks.com

Educators and librarians, for a variety of teaching tools, visit us at RHTeachersLibrarians.com

Library of Congress Cataloging-in-Publication Data is available upon request.
ISBN 978-0-593-17793-8 (trade) — ISBN 978-0-593-17794-5 (ebook)

MANUFACTURED IN CHINA
10 9 8 7 6 5 4 3 2 1
First American Edition

Avocado Asks

What am I?

by Momoko Abe

DOUBLEDAY BOOKS FOR YOUNG READERS

Avocado was feeling just fine in the
fruit and vegetable aisle of the supermarket.

Life was pretty simple. No doubts.
No questions. No confusion . . .

until one day a small
customer pointed
and asked . . .

Suddenly Avocado's world
turned upside down.

Fruit?

Vegetable?

Avocado didn't know
the answer either.

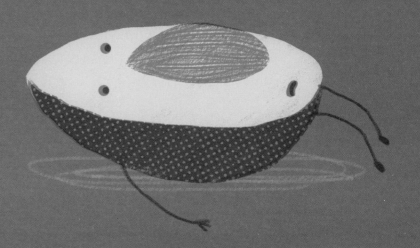

So Avocado
asked the vegetables:
"Am I a vegetable?"

The vegetables seemed confused at first,
but then the cabbages said, "You're not leafy like us."
"And you're not crunchy like us," the carrots cut in.
"And vegetables don't have a big pit in the middle,
like you do," grumbled the potatoes.

"So . . .

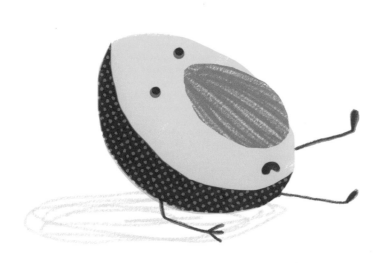

You're NOT a
VEGETABLE!

Then I must be a fruit,
thought Avocado.

So Avocado asked the fruits:
"Am I a fruit?"

"You're not sweet and juicy
like us," said the pears.
"No one would eat you as
dessert," giggled the bananas.
"You belong in a salad—
but NOT a fruit salad,"
chuckled the peaches.

Avocado's insides felt like
they were turning to guacamole.

"I don't belong with the
vegetables OR the fruit!

There must be somewhere
I can feel at home. . . .

PLEASE PAY HERE

"But where?"

Special Offer

"I'm pretty sure
I'm not an herb . . .

BASIL CHIVES THYME

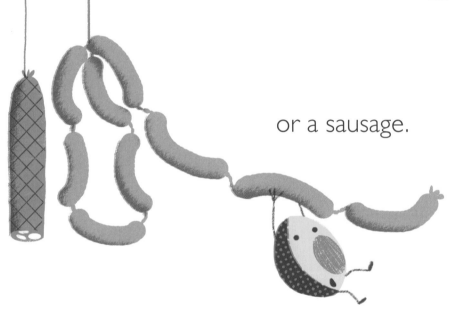

or a sausage.

I know I'm not
a canned pea
or a bean."

GARDEN PEAS GARDEN PEAS GARDEN PEAS GAR

KIDNEY BEANS KIDNEY BEANS KIDNEY BEANS KIDNEY BEANS

SWEETCORN SWEETCORN SWEETCORN SWEETCORN SWEETCORN

PLUM TOMATO PLUM TOMATO PLUM TOMATO PLUM TOMATO PLUM TOMATO

Avocado came to the fish counter. With their fins and scales, the fish looked very different. But it was worth a try.

"Am I a fish?"

"Don't be silly. Avocados can't swim," said the fish coldly.

You're NOT a
FISH!

FRESH
MACKEREL

SEASONAL
SCALLOPS

But what about the cheeses?
Some of them were ROUND, like Avocado.
Some of them had HARD SKIN on the outside too.

"Am I a cheese?" asked Avocado.

You're NOT a
CHEESE!

emmental

brie

They smell a lot like feet, thought Avocado.
I'm pretty glad I'm not a cheese. Maybe I'm an . . .

Avocado was more confused than ever.
"I'm not a fruit, a vegetable, a fish, a cheese, or an egg.

SO WHAT AM I?"

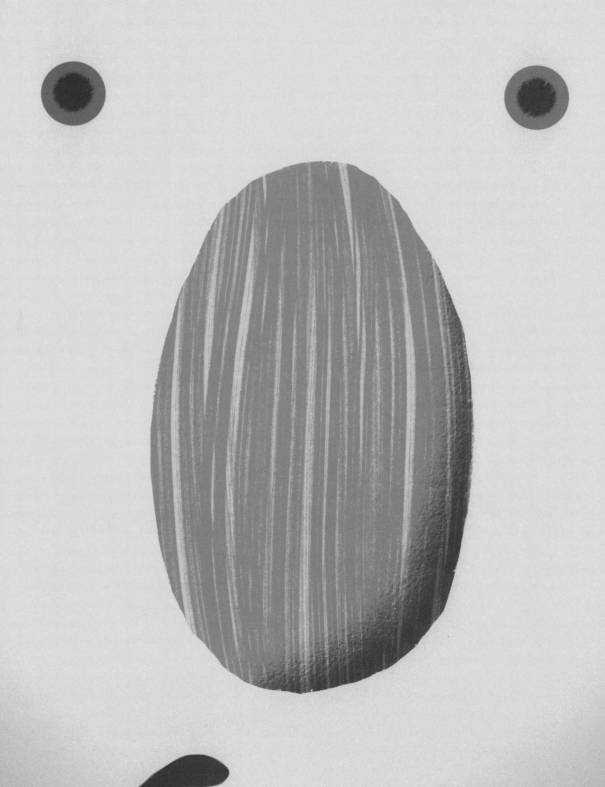

Far from the fruit and vegetable section,
Avocado was feeling lost and lonely.

And that was when
Avocado heard . . .

"Cheer up, *amigo*!" said Tomato. "You don't know what you are? So what! Don't stew in your own juices. I'm a fruit, but no one believes me.

And I. Don't. Care.

"Because I'm tasty hot or cold.

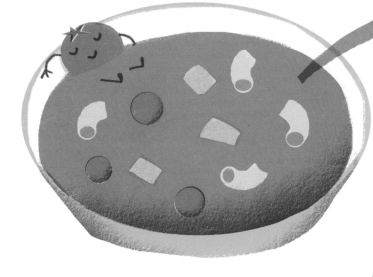

I make splendid salads and superb soup.

People love me
on pizza . . .

and adore me
with pasta.

TOMATO
KETCHUP

And they can't
get enough
of my ketchup!

And you, Avocado . . .

"You're the star
of any salad.

You're terrific
on toast and
tremendous
in tacos.

You're scrumptious
in sushi . . .

and your guacamole
is so delicious that
the other fruits and
vegetables go green
with envy.

"Who cares what we are when **we're simply AMAZING?"**

said Tomato.

It was true. They could just be themselves, and that was enough. Suddenly Avocado didn't feel lost and lonely anymore.

And that was when they heard:

Excuse me . . .